MW01077144

Maddie
THE Mitzvah
Clown
Written by
Karen Rostoker-Gruber
Illustrated by
Christine Grove

APPLES & HONEY PRESS

To Dad and Mom, who knew I was going to become
something when I grew up. . .they just didn't know what.
–K.R-G

To Molly and Gunnar, with love to the moon and back.
Forever and always.
–CG

Apples & Honey Press
An Imprint of Behrman House Publishers
Millburn, New Jersey 07041
www.applesandhoneypress.com

Text copyright © 2017 KRG Entertainment, LLC
Illustrations copyright © 2017 Apples and Honey Press

ISBN 978-1-68115-523-4

All rights reserved. No part of this publication may be translated, reproduced, stored in a retrieval system or transmitted, in any form or by any means, electronic, mechanical, photocopying, recording or otherwise, without express written permission from the publishers.

LC record available at https://lccn.loc.gov/2015051376

Project Editor: Ann D. Koffsky
Design by Zahava Bogner

Printed in China

9 8 7 6 5 4 3 2 1

0722/B1062/A4

Maddie was shy. So shy, that she felt she couldn't ask the waiter for extra cheese at her favorite restaurant.

She couldn't raise her hand at school—even if she knew the answer.

And when she went to visit Grandma at the senior home, she couldn't talk to Grandma's friends.

One day, when
Maddie was
at Grandma's,
Giggles the Mitzvah
Clown showed up.

Grandma and her friends watched Giggles make balloon hats, sing songs, juggle, and dance.

Grandma's friends laughed and laughed and laughed, and laughed some more.

After Giggles put a balloon hat on Grandma's head, the clown asked Maddie, "Would you like a balloon hat, too?"

Maddie nodded.

Giggles asked Maddie if she'd like to try on a rainbow wig.

Maddie nodded.

"And a big red nose?" Maddie nodded again and looked in the mirror.

Maddie liked how she looked with the big red nose.

Maddie liked how she looked in the rainbow wig.

And Maddie liked how the balloon hat made her smile.

Then Maddie watched Giggles talk with all of Grandma's friends.

"Maybe if I became a mitzvah clown, I could talk to Grandma's friends and make them happy—just like Giggles," Maddie thought, as she stared back into the mirror.

She didn't look or feel like herself at all.

"Can shy mice become mitzvah clowns?" asked Maddie quietly.

"Anyone can become a mitzvah clown—
even a shy mouse," said Giggles.

"My big red nose makes people laugh.
Once they start to laugh, I start to laugh.
Then we talk."

“Can you teach me how to be a mitzvah clown?” asked Maddie.

“Sure,” said Giggles.

So, over the next few weeks, Giggles taught Maddie...

how to put on clown makeup,

how to make balloon hats,

how to sing songs,

how to juggle,

how to dance,

and how to talk to and comfort everyone
in senior homes and hospitals.

Then Giggles told Maddie,
"Now you need to come up with
a clown costume."

Maddie looked in the costume trunk.

She tried on different hats, wigs, noses, shirts, pants, and shoes.

She looked in the mirror.
"What do you think?" she asked Giggles.

"You look great," said Giggles.
"Now you just need to pick a clown name.
Everyone needs to know what to call you
when they talk to you."

"How about Curly, like your wig?"

"I have a friend with that nickname," said Maddie.

"How about Big Red, like your nose?"

"It sounds like the name of a gum," said Maddie.

"How about Floppy, like your hat?"

"Maybe," said Maddie.
But none of those names seemed right for her.

Maddie paced.

And paced. And paced.

As she paced,
her shoes squeaked.

And squeaked. And squeaked.
Maddie stopped pacing.

“I’ve got it!” she said.

“I’ll be...Squeakers the Mitzvah Clown!”

“Perfect,” said Giggles.

Squeakers went on visits
to senior homes and hospitals
with Giggles and other
mitzvah clowns.

The more Squeakers visited, the less shy she became.

Squeakers made balloon hats,

Squeakers sang silly songs,

Squeakers juggled,

and Squeakers danced.

Then Squeakers tried something brave.

She took off her hat, her wig, and her big red nose...

and spoke to Grandma's friends as Maddie.

And that was the best mitzvah of all.

A Note for Families

What is a mitzvah?
A mitzvah is a Jewish commandment or obligation. It could be a good deed like visiting the sick or honoring the elderly.

What is a mitzvah clown?
A mitzvah clown is someone who dresses up in a silly costume and visits the sick or elderly. Mitzvah clowns will often make balloon animals or hats, sing songs, juggle, or dance, which helps bring cheer to the people they visit.

Is it hard to be a mitzvah clown?
It takes practice, and it might be hard at first, but it can also be fun!

For example, when Maddie puts on her clown costume and begins to sing, juggle and dance, she starts to overcome her shyness. It doesn't happen right away, but slowly, as Maddie learns how to speak with Grandma's friends, she becomes a more confident mouse—and has fun doing it!

You don't need to become a clown to do a mitzvah!

- Is there someone who you care about who isn't feeling well? How could you help cheer that person up?
- Do you have any older relatives or friends? Would they enjoy hearing from you? Could you go visit them or call them on the phone?
- Is there another mitzvah that you like to do? Does it make you happy when you do it? Why?

Giggles and happiness,
Karen Rostoker-Gruber